I WITNESSED
THE GUJARAT EARTHQUAKE

THE GUJARAT EARTHQUAKE

JOHN SMITH-SREEN

JUGGERNAUT BOOKS
C-I-128, First Floor, Sangam Vihar, Near Holi Chowk,
New Delhi 110080, India

First published by Juggernaut Books 2025

Copyright © John Smith-Sreen 2025

10 9 8 7 6 5 4 3 2 1

P-ISBN: 9789353453084
E-ISBN: 9789353459635

The views and opinions expressed in this book are the author's own. The facts contained herein were reported to be true as on the date of publication by the author to the publishers of the book, and the publishers are not in any way liable for their accuracy or veracity.

This book contains descriptions of real-life disasters and loss of life. Reader discretion is advised.

All rights reserved. No part of this publication may be reproduced, transmitted or stored in a retrieval system in any form or by any means without the written permission of the publisher.

Typeset in Futura Std by R. Ajith Kumar, Noida

Printed at Thomson Press India Ltd

*For my parents, Reginald and Elizabeth Smith,
who gave me a love of literature and adventure
and so much more.*

CONTENTS

1. Dreams — 1
2. Republic Day — 13
3. The Quake — 27
4. Trapped! — 43
5. Survival — 53
6. The Flashlight — 65
7. The Sunlight — 79
8. Recovery — 101
9. The Aftermath — 123

1
DREAMS

Seema woke with a jolt.

Her bed was *shaking*! At first, she thought she was still dreaming, but the shaking only grew stronger. In the dark, she heard water slosh in the steel cup beside her bed – SPLASH! – and then the cup tumbled onto the floor with a loud CLANG.

Seema's heart thudded. What on earth was happening?

A wail cut through the night. 'Waaaah!' It was Padma, her four-year-old sister.

Seema, seven years older and proud of never having cried since their parents had died, leapt out of bed. 'I'm coming, Padma!' she called, sprinting to the room next door.

Nani – grandmother to both girls – was just climbing out of bed. Their house was small but sturdy: walls of stabilized mud block, a concrete floor and a roof of corrugated aluminium sheets. Nana, their grandfather, had built it himself. He had worked in construction for years and always boasted, 'I know how to build a pucca house!'

Seema scooped up a trembling Padma. 'Shhh, baby, it's okay,' she whispered, even though she wasn't sure it was.

'It's an earthquake!' Nani cried. 'Quick, girls, under the bed! Your Nana built this house strong, but we must still be careful.' Then, softer, she added the line Seema had heard a thousand times: 'I only wish he were here now.'

Seema's chest tightened. Nana had disappeared months ago while working on a big house project in Bhuj. One day he simply didn't come home. Nani had begged the police for

answers and even travelled all the way to Bhuj and Ahmedabad to check hospitals and offices. Nothing. He had vanished without a trace.

How Seema missed him! Every evening, he used to share stories of his travels across Gujarat and into Rajasthan. Through his tales, Seema had fallen in love with India – even though she herself had rarely travelled outside their village of Chobari.

Nana often spoke of the Anjar Earthquake he had survived as a boy. 'The monsoon rains were pouring,' he would say, 'when the ground shook and houses crumbled.' Half the homes in Anjar collapsed because they were kutcha – flimsy and not built to standard. 'People didn't know about good foundations or reinforced mud brick,' he explained. 'Or they were too poor to build better. Many died.' That disaster had pushed him to learn proper construction so he could build strong pucca houses.

He had also drilled the family on safety. 'If an earthquake strikes, get under something solid – a table, a bed, even a strong door frame. Build well, but also be ready,' he always said. 'Be prepared.'

Remembering his advice, the sisters scrambled beneath the bed as pots and pans clattered in the kitchen.

'Nani, hurry!' Seema shouted. 'Come under with us!'

But Nani only smiled calmly. 'Not yet, beti, not yet.'

'What does that mean?' Seema cried, hugging Padma tighter. The shaking worsened; the roof groaned. 'Nani, *now*!'

'Not yet, beti, not yet,' came the serene reply.

Seema's fear turned to anger. 'If not now, then when?' she shouted over the creaking of twisting metal and the roar of the falling bricks.

'Not yet, beti, not yet,' Nani repeated.

Seema screamed – and suddenly everything went silent.

She blinked awake.

The January night in Gujarat was cool and still. The steel cup beside her bed sat full of water. No quake. No falling roof. Just a dream. A terrible, heart-pounding dream.

Seema tiptoed into the room next door. Nani snored softly. Padma slept with a faint smile on her face. Seema let out a long breath.

'Just a nightmare,' she whispered. 'But it felt so real.'

Nightmares were nothing new. Ever since the night they'd learnt of their parents' death, Seema often woke up shaking. Nani tried giving her warm milk, but the bad dreams kept coming.

To calm herself, Seema touched the cool wall beside her. Solid mud block mixed with cement – Nana's handiwork. She pictured him pressing each brick, strengthening it with steel bars and concrete beams. The house was strong. She smiled. 'Thank you, Nana,' she whispered.

And then she remembered – no school tomorrow! It was Republic Day. There would be parades, bright clothes and delicious food to share with friends. Her smile grew into a grin as she skipped back to bed.

But outside their peaceful village, trouble brewed. Kutch district was suffering from drought and rising temperatures. Nomads were moving, their goats, sheep and even camels starving for lack of fodder. People, too, were beginning to weaken.

Far beneath the sands of Kutch, hidden fault lines strained like a giant pressure cooker. Was the drought a warning? Was the heat a sign?

No one knew. Not even Seema, who drifted back to sleep on the very eve of the Great Gujarat Earthquake – an earthquake that would soon rip across Kutch, carrying people, animals and buildings with it.

And Chobari, her village, sat right on its epicentre.

2
REPUBLIC DAY

When Seema padded into the kitchen the next morning, the smell of freshly crushed spices tickled her nose. Nani was already up, working the heavy mortar and pestle she'd inherited from *her* grandmother. THUMP-THUMP – each strike of the pestle sent a puff of the fragrant masala into the air.

Padma sat on a chair, happily munching on soft, spongy yellow dhokla. 'Mmm!' she said with her mouth full.

Seema glanced up at the rows of pots and pans. Every single one hung neatly from the long nails Nana had hammered into the kitchen walls. Nothing was out of place.

Pital, copper, steel, aluminium – all gleamed in the early morning light. Nani kept them spotless even though she used them every day. Seema's favourites were the pital and copper ones, especially when the morning sun streamed through the window and made them sparkle – just like Nani's bangles.

Nani used to wear four thin gold bangles. Now she wore only two. Seema had protested when Nani had sold the other two bangles.

'You can't eat gold, beti,' Nani had said gently. 'Indian women keep gold for times of need. If we have to sell it, we do.'

Then, with a secret smile, she had shown the girls two additional bangles that she still kept hidden away. 'Don't worry,' she had promised. 'One is for your wedding, Seema, and one for Padma's.'

'Nani, garam, garam chai!' Seema called out, their usual morning greeting.

'Garam, garam chai!' echoed Padma, giggling. It was the running joke of the family.

'So, it's tea you want, eh?' Nani laughed. 'Then tea you shall have! But first, Seema, fill the kettle with water.'

Seema grabbed the kettle and dipped it into the bucket of fresh water Nani had hauled from the village hand pump at dawn. In the old days, Nani used to fetch water from the famous Chobari stepwell. She would climb carefully down the long stone steps with half the village women. Now, with the new hand pumps, the well wasn't needed for daily chores – but Seema and Padma still loved to visit.

Down near the cool water it stayed refreshingly chilly, even in the blazing pre-monsoon heat. Sometimes the sisters sat on the steps to talk about their parents.

Padma, who had been a baby when they died, only knew them through Seema's stories. Seema rarely spoke of her parents to anyone

else. Some villagers called her shy; others whispered she had grown even more quiet since the accident. Seema didn't mind. She preferred listening to talking.

Back in the kitchen, Nani lit the family's pride and joy – a shiny three-burner gas stove. Nana had bought it years ago after a successful house-building job for which the owner had rewarded the workers generously. Nana spent his bonus on the stove and a gas cylinder.

Nani usually saved the gas and cooked on dung cakes, but today was Republic Day. A little extravagance was allowed.

Soon, steaming cups of chai were ready. The three of them – grandmother and granddaughters – sat together, sipping tea and soaking up the warm morning. Since their parents' death, Seema and Nani had become especially close. And little Padma barely remembered a time when Nani and Seema weren't her entire world.

'What shall we do to celebrate Republic Day, my dears?' Nani asked. 'Shall we travel to Bhuj and see the parade? We could take the bus and roam around the town all day.'

Seema's smile faded. Padma's too. Their parents had been killed in a bus accident returning from Ahmedabad. The driver, chewing paan and running on little food, had been forced to drive one more route after a long shift. Some survivors said he had been speeding. Others thought he had fallen asleep.

Seema and Padma's parents died instantly. Others suffered for hours before help arrived in the remote corner of Kutch.

'Nani, let's stay in Chobari,' Seema said softly. 'There may not be a parade like in Bhuj, but we can still enjoy the village festivities – and all the savoury food you're making!'

'Yes, yes!' Padma piped up. 'And sweets!'

'Alright, my dears,' Nani agreed with a smile. 'Chobari it is. I'll buy a few things from

the market so we can cook a real Republic Day feast in Nana's house. But first, let's seek Lord Shiva's blessings.'

The girls grinned. Every morning Nani visited the village mandir to pray to Mahadev, and Seema loved to go with her. Following Nani, Seema always touched the Nandi bull statue before stepping into the inner sanctum where the Shiva lingam rested. Today, she also paused at the small shrine of Goddess Durga.

Seema felt a special connection to Durga – ten arms holding weapons, a fierce lion at her feet, yet a calm, serene face. The goddess's strength and kindness wrapped Seema in a protective glow.

With Padma beside her, Seema prayed devotedly for Mother India on this Republic Day.

Neither of them knew that deep beneath the sands of Kutch, the earth was already stirring.

Before the morning was over the Gujarat Earthquake would erupt. Chobari would

lie frighteningly close to the epicentre of an earthquake that would prove to be one of the deadliest ever to strike India. But for now, the girls and their grandmother prayed in peace, unaware that the ground itself was getting ready to roar.

3
THE QUAKE

The girls returned home and Nani set off towards the Chobari market, her grocery basket swinging at her side. She passed the village's huge water tower and nodded to herself. *Progress,* she thought. With the big tank and the freshly renovated market, Chobari was doing well.

At home, she kept plenty of dry lentils and flour, stacked in steel tins beside her beloved pots and pans. She had already ground spices that morning. Now she needed fresh things: tomatoes, onions, ginger, coriander and green chillies for the dal. She wanted to cook something special for her granddaughters.

If she found fresh fenugreek leaves, she'd make thepla – the girls' favourite Gujarati flatbread. If there were pigeon peas, she'd turn them into lilva kachori – little stuffed dumplings the girls loved. And on the way back she'd buy jalebis so they'd still be hot when she reached home.

Then Nani felt . . . odd.

As if the ground had tilted, just a little. She staggered. The world swam. Nani wondered why she suddenly felt dizzy and unsteady.

She didn't know that deep underground – seventeen kilometres deep – huge plates were shifting. New faults were forming. Destruction was coming, swift and terrible. It would kill, injure and destroy.

The first rumble hit.

Nani dropped to her knees with a cry. Shouts burst from the market. People screamed from nearby houses. The tall, vertical water

tank shuddered – and CRASHED – splitting open with a roar. Water burst out in waves, drenching Nani and rushing in small streams down Chobari's streets.

She tried to stand, water dripping from her hair. She managed to get up on one shaky knee – and then the ground buckled. The shaking surged. WHAM! Nani was sent sprawling on the dirt road. She tried again and again, but the quake slammed her down, roaring like an angry demon, tossing her from one side of the lane to the other.

'Lord Shiva, protect me,' she prayed. 'Protect Seema and Padma!'

The road began to roll and whip, like laundry on a clothesline flapping in the wind. Houses around her started to crumble. The market's new pillars and roof – the ones the panchayat had just renovated – collapsed in a cloud of dust and noise.

My fenugreek leaves! flashed through Nani's mind, and then she scolded herself – *no, my girls!*

She screamed with all her might, 'Seema, quick – it is an earthquake! It is time! It is time!'

She was far too distant for Seema to hear, but Nani was in shock – thinking only of fear and love. 'It is time!' she cried again, voice cracking, and crumpled to the shaking ground.

She tried once more to push up, stubborn as ever. The quake hurled her down, face-first into the dust. She had to reach her girls – she *had* to – but the next violent jolt slammed her so hard she lost consciousness. Around her, buildings kept collapsing as the quake roared on and on.

Back at the house, Seema was sipping her second cup of tea. Padma sat beside her, playing with a toy set a kind neighbour – an excellent craftsman – had made: a brightly

dressed pair of dolls with sticks in their hands. Padma made them whirl and tap as if they were doing a garba dance.

The first tremor made the cup twitch. Tea sloshed over the rim – slurp – spill – and the shaking increased.

Wait. Am I dreaming again? Seema thought for one dizzy second.

Then Padma's dolls clattered to the floor. The little girl lifted her arms towards her sister, eyes wide with worry – then fear. On the kitchen wall, Nani's pots and pans leapt from their hooks – CLANG! CLATTER! – and steel tins of lentils pinged across the floor. This was no dream. It was an earthquake.

Through the booming and rattling, Seema heard her grandmother's voice, loud as a bell in her mind: 'It is time! It is time!'

And then her grandfather's voice too: 'Be prepared! Be ready when catastrophe strikes.'

Seema scooped up her sister. With her free hand she grabbed the open tin of dhokla from the counter. She snatched a bottle of drinking water. 'Quick, Padma – like Nana told us! Under something strong!' she shouted, racing into Nani's bedroom.

Padma wriggled on her belly under the big wooden double bed – solid and heavy, built by Nana himself. Seema shoved the dhokla tin and the water bottle after her. *What else?* Her eyes darted around – there! A cheap Chinese flashlight on the bedside. She grabbed it without thinking.

'It is time!' Nani's voice urged inside her head. Seema ducked under the bed just as a huge tremor hit. The whole house lurched. Mud blocks thudded down. From under the frame, she saw daylight knifing in from the front room – oh no! A section of the front wall must have fallen.

Seema hugged Padma close, trying to hush her screams. The floor heaved like a boat in

rough water. Outside came a low, endless rumble, the smash of collapsing buildings and the cries of neighbours. Nausea rolled through Seema with every sickening wave of the concrete slab – but still Nana's house stood strong.

Dust choked the room. Seema pulled off her dupatta and wrapped it around Padma's face, trying to filter the grit. The noise, the dust, the wild shaking – and Padma's terrified sobs – didn't stop. Still Nana's house stood strong.

The earthquake was relentless, an angry drum that wouldn't quit. The chaos went on and on, flattening whatever lay in its path. Then, just when the girls thought they couldn't bear another second, the shaking built up even more. A full minute – more – of punishing jolts surged and ebbed. In the kitchen, pots and pans lay everywhere. The beloved cook stove was twisted at a crooked angle. Still Nana's house stood strong.

Another half minute. The quake reached a fever pitch – an awful, roaring crescendo.

Heavy stabilized mud blocks ripped from the walls. The concrete ring beam that tied the house together cracked – KR-RAKK! – and crumbled, chunks splitting away. The roof girders twisted and went SNAP! SNAP! – like twigs in the wind.

Under the bed, the sisters clutched each other and prayed to Goddess Durga for protection. The floor bucked beneath them. The roof screamed. Then, with one last thunderous roar, Nana's house gave way – collapsing in a storm of dust and debris, burying Nani's shining pital pots and pans, the great wooden bed . . .

and the girls beneath.

4

TRAPPED!

It was black.

Not just night-time black – but the kind of black where you can't tell if your eyes are open or shut.

Seema couldn't see her own hand, let alone Padma. But she could *feel* her little sister's trembling body and hear her frightened whimpers. Dust clogged the air, thick and scratchy. Even with the dupatta pulled across their faces, it clawed at their throats and noses, trying to force its way into their lungs.

Seema thought in horror, *this dust is trying to snuff out our breath.*

Panic surged inside her chest like a second earthquake. The deafening roar of the quake had stopped, but now the silence was somehow worse – huge, heavy, almost loud enough to hurt.

Padma squirmed in Seema's arms and let out a long, mournful wail that broke into short, sharp sobs. The darkness, the dust, the choking air – it was too much. Seema fought to stay calm, but the fear kept rising. They were trapped. They couldn't breathe.

A small cry escaped Seema's throat. Padma screamed back, her panic feeding Seema's own.

And then – Nana's voice, clear as if he were right beside her: 'Be ready. Be prepared.'

The familiar words steadied her. Seema fumbled across the floor until her fingers touched something smooth and plastic – the cheap flashlight she'd grabbed. She clicked it on.

A weak yellow beam cut through the blackness. Light!

Seema and Padma stared at each other, eyes wide but hearts a little calmer. Padma's

sobs softened into hiccupping whimpers. Seema tugged the dupatta from their faces and managed a shaky smile.

'We're alive, Padma,' she whispered. 'We're alive. Mother Durga heard our prayers.'

Padma threw her arms around her sister. 'Please, Didi,' she whispered, 'let's go. Let's go find Nani.'

Seema shone the torch around their tiny hiding space. She spotted the water bottle and the tin of dhokla. The dhokla was coated in dust, but she poured a little water into her palm and helped Padma sip, clearing the grit from her throat and nose.

The girls studied their surroundings in the glow of the torch. Four sturdy wooden legs held up the bed above them, its slats stuffed with soft silk–cotton fibres Nani refreshed every year. Everywhere else lay huge chunks of mud brick, some whole, some broken. Seema pushed

against one block. It didn't budge. They were well and truly trapped.

'Help!' Seema shouted.

'Help! Help!' echoed Padma. 'Help!'

Only silence answered.

Padma's eyes welled up again. Seema stroked her cheek. 'Shhh, my baby. We'll be alright. Nani will come for us soon.'

She offered Padma more water and broke off a tiny piece of dhokla from the clean bottom of the tin. 'Here, Padma Rani,' she said gently. 'Eat a little. It will keep your strength up.'

Padma chewed the spongy bite and whispered, 'Thank you, Didi. Where's Nani? I want Nani.'

Seema hugged her close. 'She'll come,' she said, though her own voice trembled.

Far from the ruins of their house, though, their grandmother lay face-down in the dirt, surrounded by death and destruction. As far

as anyone could see, not a single building in Chobari remained standing.

Nana's house – the house that had stood longer than all the rest – had been the very last to fall.

5
SURVIVAL

Seema knew they were lucky to be alive – and she was determined to keep it that way. But how? How would they get out? Where was Nani? Where were the neighbours? Why hadn't anyone come?

Time inside their tiny prison felt slippery and strange. Minutes? Hours? They couldn't tell how long had passed. Their world was now the size of a double bed, a low box of wood and rubble. They couldn't sit up. They couldn't even kneel. Both sisters lay flat on their bellies, able to wiggle only a few feet in any direction.

Seema had tried turning off the flashlight to save its weak batteries, but the instant darkness sent Padma into a panic. With a sigh, Seema switched it back on. The thin beam glowed like a lifeline.

She pushed at the mud blocks hemming them in, fingers scrabbling for grip. The bricks were huge and heavy. Nana had mixed cement into the mud to make them strong – too strong. Seema's fingernails split, her palms bled, but the blocks refused to move. Her own cries of frustration made Padma's eyes go wide, so Seema bit back her tears.

'Finish the rest of the dhokla, baby,' she said instead. 'Even the dusty pieces. You must keep your strength up.'

'But what about you, Didi? You need strength too.' Seema pretended to nibble a piece so Padma would eat. Between Seema's fake bites and Padma's real ones, the dhokla disappeared – dust and all.

What Seema really wanted was the tin itself. The edge was sharp enough to scrape

against the mud bricks. She gripped it tight and began chiselling at the nearest block, the metal screeching softly as she worked.

'We're in prison,' Padma whispered.

'No, baby,' Seema said quickly. 'This is our sanctuary. From here we can travel anywhere we want. Where shall we go? Bhuj? Jaipur? Delhi?'

She made her voice rise with each city name, as if they were boarding a magical train.

'Delhi!' Padma giggled.

Neither girl had ever left Gujarat, but Seema had heard plenty of stories – at school, in the village and especially from Nana, who had travelled to the capital several times. So, while she scraped and scraped, Seema spun pictures with her words. She described Shah Jahan's magnificent Red Fort, the graceful arches of Humayun's Tomb, the soaring Jama Masjid and the grand Rajpath leading to the India Gate.

Padma's eyes gleamed in the dusty light, her mind flying far above the rubble.

Outside, the real Delhi lay hundreds of kilometres away, and the afternoon sun shone on a scene of heartbreak. Chobari's streets were choked with debris – shattered mud bricks, twisted aluminium roofing, splintered rafters, even bodies. Some villagers wandered in shock. Others searched desperately for loved ones or tried to dig survivors from the ruins. The health centre lay in pieces; the village nurse was missing. No one yet understood that the quake had ravaged all of western Gujarat and even shaken parts of Pakistan.

Back under the bed, Seema kept scraping. Her hands were raw, the tin slick with blood, but she never let Padma see her pain. Nana's strong bricks were proving too strong, each cement-hardened block resisting her every effort.

Still, she worked, talking of Delhi's wonders, promising that one day they would see them together.

Then – movement! A block shifted. Seema's heart leapt. She pushed again. Another shift.

She rolled onto her back, planted her feet against the stubborn brick and shoved with all her might. The block slid. Daylight! A sliver of sky shone through the dust.

'We're free!' Seema gasped.

'Oh Didi!' Padma squealed.

But before they could squeeze through, the ground shuddered again.

An aftershock – sharp and merciless – sent more bricks crashing down. The narrow opening was sealed in an instant.

Seema yanked her hand back just in time, but the precious dhokla tin – her only tool – was crushed beneath the new pile of rubble.

They were trapped once more, their small window to the outside world slammed shut.

6

THE FLASHLIGHT

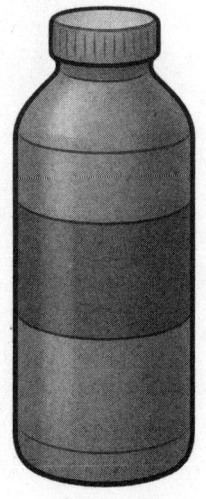

Seema was dead tired. Her arms felt like they might drop right off her body. She couldn't scrape another inch – especially now that her trusty dhokla tin was gone.

She flopped onto her back and shoved at the stubborn blocks with her legs. Nothing. Not even a tiny wiggle. A small cry of frustration escaped before she could stop it.

'What is it, Didi?' wailed Padma. 'What's wrong?'

'It's nothing, my baby,' Seema said quickly. 'Don't worry. I just need to change positions so I can dig some more. See?' She rolled onto her belly and began scraping again with her fingernails.

Her hands were locked like claws; every move was agony. But she refused to cry out. She refused to give up. The flashlight's weak beam was fading, its glow now a dull, sickly yellow.

'Padma Rani,' Seema said softly, forcing cheer into her voice. 'When should we visit Delhi? Maybe during the school holidays? What do you think?'

Padma blinked at her sister, unsure how to answer. She was bone tired too. They had been lying under the bed for what felt like forever, trapped in a space no bigger than the bed itself. Why hadn't Nani come? Where were the neighbours?

Seema started to sing – a soft lullaby their mother used to hum. Padma's eyes fluttered closed, and soon she was asleep. Seema gazed at her sister's peaceful face, love and exhaustion mixing until her own eyelids drooped. *A quick nap*, she thought. *Just a quick one.*

When she woke, she whispered urgently, 'Here, Padma. Take another sip of water.'

Padma gulped greedily. Though it was January, the afternoons in Kutch could grow warm, and the fallen mud blocks had sealed them inside a brick oven. Sweat soaked their clothes. Seema knew they should ration their water, but she couldn't bring herself to stop her sister from drinking.

The flashlight flickered weakly. It had been on for hours – longer than Seema could count. That cheap green plastic torch made in China had become their one loyal friend. Seema felt a shiver of dread. If the light died, would they, too?

Determined, she dug again, her raw fingers carving a shallow groove between two wedged blocks.

Then the ground rumbled. Before either girl could react, the floor bucked upwards, slamming their heads into the wooden slats above. Both screamed as an aftershock shook the earth.

Seema clutched the flickering torch. It shook because *she* was shaking. But when the

tremor faded, the light steadied – and to their amazement, glowed brighter than before.

In the stronger beam, Padma's eyes caught a flash of silver. 'Didi! Look!' she squeaked, pointing.

Something shiny peeked from the rubble. Seema crawled over. The dhokla tin! The aftershock had shifted the blocks just enough for it to show.

It was wedged tight, but Seema tugged and twisted, working it back and forth. At last, with a final grunt, she pulled it free. Both girls burst out laughing as if greeting an old friend. The tin was flattened like a dosa, but Seema didn't care. She had a tool again!

She scraped furiously, no longer tearing her nails. Thirty minutes passed. The torch dimmed to a sickly flicker. Seema gave it a hard shake – CLICK! – and it flared back to life.

Flicker, shake, light. Flicker, shake, light. The pattern continued all afternoon as Seema

scraped and clawed, then flipped onto her back to push with her feet.

'Wait – did that block just move?' Her heart skipped. She pushed again, little legs straining. Yes! It moved!

Seema flipped onto her belly and kept scraping, finding a rhythm: scrape, flip, push. Scrape, flip, push.

Then, disaster.

A final shove made the block slide – and with it, the fragile pile above collapsed. Chunks of mud brick tumbled down and pinned Seema's legs.

She cried out in pain and fear.

'Didi!' Padma screamed. 'Are you okay?'

Seema grimaced. The weight crushed her legs. She tried to sit up, but the bed slats pressed her flat. It hurt. It really hurt.

'Padma Rani, you'll have to unbury me,' Seema said, her voice calmer than she felt. 'You can do it. I know you can.'

Little Padma began lifting chunks of brick, one by one. Slow at first, then faster as Seema cheered her on. 'Try to hurry, Padma Rani,' Seema said, stifling a scream. The pain in her legs was unbearable. Piece by piece, the pressure eased. At last, Seema pulled one leg free, then the other.

She hugged her sister tight. 'Good job, my brave one.'

Then, without resting, she grabbed the dented tin and went back to work.

The flicker–shake–light routine carried on: scrape, scrape, scrape, pray, push, scrape. Each push made a tiny bit of progress. A small gap appeared near one of the bedposts. But Seema worked carefully, afraid to trigger another collapse.

The sisters began calling out together: 'Help! Help us!'

Their voices echoed in the sealed chamber, but no one answered.

It wasn't that no one cared. Outside, chaos ruled. The village lay in ruins. So many were dead or injured – including their beloved Nani – that even those who survived barely knew where to begin.

Still, under the crushed remains of Nana's house, two small sisters refused to give up.

7

THE SUNLIGHT

A few more scrapes. A few more shoves. And then – light.

A thin beam of afternoon sun slipped through a gap between Nana's blocks. Seema and Padma both gasped.

'Oh, Didi!' Padma cried. 'You did it!'

'We did it, Padma Rani,' Seema whispered back. 'You dug me out so I could dig you out.' Her eyes stung – half dust, half happy tears. *Thank you, Mother Durga,* she prayed silently.

The flashlight finally died with a sad little flicker – pfft! – but the girls barely noticed. Sunlight bounced into their tiny cave as Seema hurried to widen the hole.

All morning and into the afternoon, Nani had lain on the road. At last, a neighbour found her and helped her up. Her head throbbed; the world tilted. *How long was I out?* she wondered.

She drifted through what used to be Chobari, stepping over rubble, then — heart twisting — stepping over people. Everywhere she looked she saw the same scene: broken mud bricks, twisted roofs, splintered rafters. Her beloved village was gone. *Where are my girls? Where are Seema and Padma?*

The ground around her squelched. Water. She remembered being drenched. She looked up and saw the shattered water tower, toppled on its side. Yes — she'd passed it on the way to market that morning. If this was the tower . . . then *home* was that way.

Nani started towards the market. The big roof there had collapsed; concrete pillars lay crooked beneath bent sheets of corrugated aluminium. Before she could go farther, the earth reared

again. WHUMP! An aftershock flung her down. She staggered up, took two steps – THUD! Another tremor slammed her into the dust. When the ground calmed, she dragged herself upright and tried to think. Morning. Market. *Home is this way.* She turned and walked.

But every landmark was gone. Every lane looked like a new one made of rubble. Nani's throat burned with thirst. The late afternoon sun was setting. *Had she really lain in the street all day?*

'Where is my house?' she wailed. 'Where are my children?'

A small boy slipped his hand into hers. Nani recognized him – Arjan, the neighbour's child who lived close by. He didn't speak. He just tugged her along the broken lanes, around heaps of brick and roof. They turned into a narrow passage that felt familiar. Arjan stopped beside a tall mound of mud blocks and twisted aluminium. He looked up and smiled. Nani

stared back, confused – then she understood. This was her house. Or what was left of it. A howl tore out of her chest. Startled, the boy darted away.

'Oh, beta, I'm sorry!' she called – but he was gone.

Nani scoured the pile for a sign of the girls. She tried to lift a brick – too heavy. She could shift it a little, not move it away. 'Seema! Padma! It's me. I've come back!' Silence pressed in.

A flash caught her eye. Something bright, half-buried. Nani dug it free – her old pital karahi, dented but sound. She clutched the sturdy pan like a friend returned from war. Sunlight glinted off the brass, and the reflection danced across the highest part of the rubble, right over the centre.

Then – was that a sound? A faint voice? Scratching?

'Seema!' Nani shouted. 'Are you there?'

Scritch. Scritch-scritch. The sound grew louder. A tiny hole appeared – exactly where the reflected light was shining. The hole widened. Wider.

'Nani! Nani!' a voice called from inside.

'Oh, meri jaan!' Nani cried. 'You are here! You are alive!'

The sun hit the pital just right and shot a bright beam through the opening, pouring light into the space beneath the bed. Warmth. Comfort. Hope.

Seema squinted out, blinking at the glare. 'I knew you'd come, Nani,' she called. 'I prayed to Mother Durga. I knew she would protect us.'

'I knew you'd come too!' Padma shouted. 'I also prayed!'

'We hid under the bed – just like Nana told us,' Seema added.

'I knew you'd be under the bed,' Nani answered, voice shaking with pride. 'You are truly my clever Seema. Both my clever girls.' She

cried – but only for a heartbeat. Then she wiped her cheeks and tried, once more, to move the blocks. Too heavy.

'I need help,' she told herself. 'But how will I find my way back?' Her little guide had run off. And he had looked like *he* needed help too.

Nani tore her shawl in half. She tied one piece to a wooden rafter sticking out of the debris. 'Seema, Padma,' she called, 'I will return very quickly with strong men to get you out. I promise.'

'We'll be here,' Seema replied, trying to sound brave.

'Don't go, Nani!' Padma cried.

Nani's heart pulled towards them, but she forced herself to move. Down the lane, she tied the second shawl piece to a twisted roofing sheet. Then she saw a woman crushed beneath a fallen wall – still, silent. Nani bowed her head. 'Forgive me, bahin-ji,' she whispered, gently slipping the woman's dupatta free. She tore it

into four strips and tied one at each turn in the path. She did the same with other dupattas she found, marking a clear breadcrumb trail from her home to the market square.

There, a crowd had gathered. Some dug with bare hands. Some called names into holes. 'Help!' Nani cried. 'Help – my girls need help!'

Six strong men hurried to her. She told them everything in a rush. They followed her fluttering trail of dupatta flags back to the ruin of Nana's house.

'Seema! Padma! I'm back with help!' Nani called.

'We are here, Nani,' came Seema's answer.

'Thank you, Nani!' piped Padma.

The men studied the mound, then began carefully lifting bricks around the small opening. Slowly. Gently. Any wrong move and the pile could slide, burying the girls. Inch by inch the gap grew.

A dusty head popped up – Padma! Hair sticking every which way, grin as wide as

Gujarat. The men laughed and cheered despite everything. They passed her down, from one person to the next, until she tumbled into Nani's arms.

Seema was next. Her head fit through the opening – but her shoulders got jammed. She wriggled. A man tugged. No luck. She slid back, tried again – one arm first, then her head. Still stuck.

She pushed with her legs; a man pulled her arm. Pain flared – her poor hands were shredded – but she moved a few inches. Then – stuck tight. Wouldn't go forward, wouldn't go backward.

'Be patient, beti!' Nani called. 'We'll get you out.'

'Nana always said *be prepared*, Nani, not *be patient*!' Seema shot back.

Even now – teasing! Nani blinked hard. *The human spirit*, she thought. *Look at my girl.*

Then Seema's voice turned serious. 'Be prepared, Nani – can you find the ghee?'

Nani frowned, then understood. She scrambled over to the wrecked kitchen. Near where she had found the karahi sat the toppled urn of ghee she used for cooking and spreading on chapatis. A few dollops were still inside.

She hauled it back. The men slathered the ghee along Seema's sides. The slippery butter ran down her arms. Seema twisted; the men pulled. One shoulder slid free, then the other. Her waist cleared, then her hips – and suddenly she was out, sprinting straight into Nani's arms.

Padma already clung to Nani; now all three clutched one another – ghee, dust, blood and all – laughing and crying at the same time. They thanked the men again and again and bowed their heads in prayer to Lord Shiva and Mother Durga.

Then Nani took a proper look at Seema. Hands and forearms criss-crossed with cuts and

scrapes. Fingernails shattered. Blood on her legs from when the rubble had pinned her – wounds Seema had barely noticed.

One of the men had wisely brought a roll of medical gauze. Nani filled the karahi with water at the village hand pump and came back to clean each wound. 'Oh, my brave, brave girl,' she cooed, wrapping neat white bandages around all four limbs.

'Seema saved us, Nani,' Padma said, eyes wet. 'She dug with a tin – and when the tin was lost, she dug with her hands. Look at her poor hands.'

'Ah, but you saved me too,' Seema said gently. 'Who dug me out when the blocks fell on my legs?'

'I did,' Padma whispered, cheeks pink. 'But you really saved us.'

A small head peeked around the corner – Arjan, the little guide. Nani beckoned him close and wrapped him in a grateful hug. He hugged

her back, then slipped his hand into Padma's and began telling her a very serious, very four-year-old story.

And for the first time that terrible day, the sun felt warm again.

8
RECOVERY

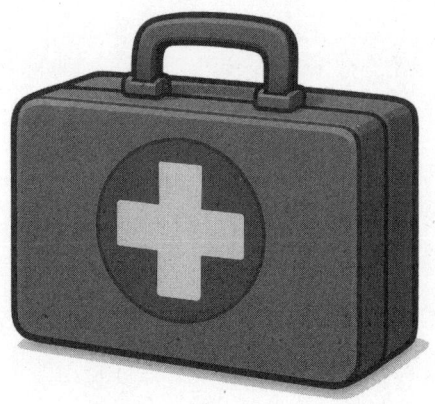

Non-governmental organizations – NGOs – were fast.

Teams rushed into Chobari, Bhuj and nearby villages to help survivors and gather the dead. The central and state governments followed quickly. NGO teams worked with government workers and good-hearted neighbours on urgent rescues, and also began planning for the long road of recovery. The international community was alerted, and they sent support. India's own capable NGOs were everywhere – some had arrived within hours of the quake.

That night, Nani led Seema to a medical tent that had popped up in the village. A doctor checked her carefully. Bandages removed; wound cleaned, disinfected, re-dressed. The doctor felt for broken bones and looked for signs of internal bleeding. Verdict: serious cuts and scrapes on the hands, arms and legs; all fingernails torn and splintered from clawing at the blocks; fingertips bloodied and raw; deep bruises on both legs from the falling debris – but no fractures.

Padma sat pressed against Seema the whole time, chattering to the doctor. 'We were trapped under the bed and Seema saved us,' she reported proudly.

'You're lucky to have such an ingenious sister,' the doctor said with a smile.

'I know, I know,' Padma answered, puffing up with pride. Nani's eyes shone. She also felt proud – and very lucky.

Outside the tent, the doctor had many more patients. Some had broken bones or crushed limbs. Some lay on blankets, moaning. Others

stared upwards, silent, eyes empty. Seema could not tell who was alive.

An NGO worker handed them blankets and bottled water. Now, where to sleep? Nowhere, really. Night fell, but the levelled village still buzzed with people picking through the pieces of their lives. In the end, Nani and the girls returned to their flattened home. They cleared a patch of floor where the kitchen had been and lay down. Sleep came in bits and pieces. Padma woke again and again, crying out, and Seema soothed her. 'Shush, baby. It's okay. We're safe now. Nani is here.'

Morning brought a surprising sight: rescue crews from Japan, Turkey and the United States working side by side with volunteers from Chobari and the state government, digging and digging.

Seema spotted the six men who had pulled her and Padma out; they had worked all night, moving blocks, stacking roof tiles, tugging neighbours from the ruins.

Many able-bodied villagers joined in. Those who could dig, dug. Others handed out supplies or helped NGO staff organize the work. The whole village pitched in. Seema watched the foreign rescue dogs – noses down, tails stiff – sniffing the piles and barking to call crews over. Too often, the find was a body. But sometimes – sometimes – someone was alive.

Whenever a survivor was freed – wide-eyed, dust-grey, shaking – Seema hurried over. 'I was buried too,' she'd say softly. 'You will be okay.' Some people could not answer. Some simply cried. Seema stayed anyway. Padma helped in her own way, her small hand warm in a stranger's palm while medics checked them over.

Seema began learning the names on the vests and trucks: CARE, Catholic Relief Services, Oxfam. She noticed the United Nations teams in blue hats and vests, putting up tents and organizing food, water and medical points. She was glad to see Indian groups so active initially

in the rescue operations and eventually in the recovery efforts. She was especially pleased to see women from SEWA – Self Employed Women's Association in Ahmedabad – who began helping other women rebuild livelihoods after homes and shops were lost.

A foreigner spoke to Nani, and soon a mixed team – people from Chobari and from outside – started pitching tents. Nani and the girls were assigned one, a big step up from the kitchen floor. Someone from Janpath Citizen's Initiative sat with Nani and Seema, noting their experiences and needs.

A truck groaned to a stop near the tents. Supplies! Seema helped Nani carry a case of drinking water and a case of biscuits. She also claimed a box of tiny packets – Oral Rehydration Salts. She mixed one into a bottle and handed it to Padma before the biscuits, even when the complaints began. They had eaten only dhokla yesterday; Nani had eaten nothing. She knew

Padma was hungry, but quenching her thirst was more important.

Padma, truth be told, didn't mind the salty drink – she was *so* thirsty – but complaining was part of being four. Seema just hugged her and passed her the Marie biscuits. 'But Seema Didi, I prefer Parle-G,' Padma giggled. Seema raised a hand in pretend scolding, then pulled her in for another squeeze. Nani watched them with a soft smile.

A small face peeped into the tent – the neighbour boy. Padma shared her biscuits with him. 'His name is Arjan,' she informed Nani and Seema. 'And he can't find his mother. He has no father either.'

Nani took Arjan's hand. 'Come, let's look,' she said. His eyes went wide, hopeful. The three of them, plus Seema, set out.

At Arjan's home – or what was left of it – Nani asked gently, 'Are you sure this is your house, Arjan?' There was almost nothing: a heap of

dust and thatch. Arjan nodded. Tears slipped down his cheeks.

Padma made soft cooing sounds and hugged him. 'Don't worry, Arjan. We'll keep looking.'

Seema was glad she didn't promise *we'll find her*. Bodies lay everywhere. No one could promise anything today.

They searched and searched, following Nani's dupatta scraps and circling back. No luck.

An NGO worker took down the details. Arjan didn't know his mother's first name, but he did know his own surname. The worker promised to add it to the database his organization was building.

'Can Arjan stay with us, Nani? Please?' Padma asked. Arjan stood very still, hopeful and sad.

'Would you like that, Arjan?' Nani asked. He nodded hard – more energy than he'd shown

all day. 'Then it's settled,' Nani said warmly. 'Come live with us for now.'

The sisters hugged him. That night they all returned to the tent together. Arjan's mother was never found. And that is how Arjan became Seema and Padma's brother, a cherished part of their family.

Later, Seema wanted to go back to the site of their house. There was nothing left, but maybe something could be salvaged. Nani still had her cooking pot; beyond the clothes on their backs, a few biscuits and water, that was it. Also, Seema wanted to see the bed. Their shelter. Their lifesaver.

Padma and Arjan wanted to come too, and Nani refused to let them out of her sight, so all four went.

They followed the torn dupatta trail. As they neared the house, they saw a group of men hauling and stacking Nana's blocks.

'What are you doing there?' Seema called. 'That is our house!'

Nani blinked. Seema speaking first – to strangers! *What has gotten into that child?* she thought.

'This is very good building material,' one man explained. 'Our NGO will build new houses for Chobari. We'll take these blocks to start the foundations.'

'It is good building material,' Seema shot back, 'because my Nana made it. You can start by building a new house here before you take any of Nana's bricks!'

Nani chuckled. 'That's my girl!'

The men conferred with each other, pointing at the plot where the house had stood. Heads shook, then nodded. Decision made. 'Alright, alright – you have a deal. Your Nana chose a good site. We'll rebuild right here for you.'

'And I'll be here to make sure you do good work,' Seema said, hands on her hips. 'Nana

had very high standards — and you will follow them.' Nani cackled. The NGO representative laughed good-naturedly.

All day the men worked — stacking good blocks, clearing unusable rubble. From a safe distance, Nani, Seema, Padma and Arjan watched, then darted in to rescue anything that appeared: a pair of leather chappals, one of Padma's blue skirts with red appliqué, a dented steel cup and — hooray! — a blouse and skirt for Seema. Dusty, yes. But better than what she was wearing.

Slowly, the bed emerged.

Seema stepped forward. She ran her hand along the foot board, then down the side, past the jagged hole out of which she and Padma had crawled to freedom. At the headboard's corner post, she patted the wood and smiled.

The NGO representative came close and spoke softly. 'Aren't you the girl who survived by

sheltering under this bed? With your sister? How did you know what to do? Who taught you?'

Seema gave the smallest nod. 'Nana,' she whispered.

The men finished freeing the bed. Then, carefully, almost reverently, they carried it over and set it down for everyone to sit on.

'I love this bed,' Padma announced. 'But I love the topside better than the bottom.' Laughter burst out – real, ringing laughter – until tears ran down their dusty cheeks.

9

THE AFTERMATH

Once Nana's house was built again, the NGO worker came to visit. He liked the strong walls and neat work. The new house was even better than before. Seema and Nani had given some ideas, and the team had used new earthquake-safe methods.

Then the NGO worker shared some big news. Because Seema had pushed to work with the NGO, they had decided to try a new method: owner-driven reconstruction. That meant families helping to plan and rebuild their own homes. This idea was spreading across Gujarat. Seema was amazed – her words had changed how houses were built!

Then the worker shared some even bigger news. But he spoke with Nani first. When she agreed, he spoke to Seema.

'At first,' he said, 'we helped right after the quake – finding missing people, treating injuries and helping with funerals for families.

'Then we focused on food, water and shelter. We set up tents. After that, we rebuilt pucca houses using earthquake-safe methods, like your Nana taught – always working with the families who would live there. You know this – you lived it.

'Now we must do more. People's bodies are healing, but their hearts and minds are still hurting. We need to help them be strong again. Disasters will come and go. We must be prepared.'

'Yes!' Seema said. 'We need long-term plans. We must be ready when disaster strikes. That's what my Nana always said.'

'Exactly,' he smiled. 'Your Nana was wise – and a good builder.'

Seema beamed.

'This is where you come in,' he said. 'We need to meet people and talk about earthquakes, and other disasters too. People need clear information so they can change what they do and be safer. They can learn from you. You were ready. You stayed smart. Your grandfather built a strong house. And you survived. Tell your story so others can be ready. We'll travel across Gujarat and meet many groups.'

Nani looked at Seema. Padma looked at Seema. Even Arjan looked at Seema. Seema had once feared talking to strangers and leaving Chobari. Now, she was being asked to speak to big groups all over the state.

'This could save lives, Seema,' the worker added.

'Yes – oh, yes! I can do this!' she said.

A few weeks after the quake, the shy girl from Chobari started speaking for the NGO

across Gujarat. The worker gave her facts and numbers. Twenty thousand people had died that day – mostly in the north-west of Gujarat – and the damage had even reached Sindh in Pakistan. There were 167,000 people who were badly hurt; over a million homes were destroyed, and 1.7 million people lost their homes in a moment.

People also called it the Bhuj Earthquake because Bhuj, a large town, was hit hard. The quake had struck on 26 January 2001, in the morning. The epicentre – the starting point underground – was about 20 kilometres north-west of Bhuj.

Much of Kutch was badly damaged. Chobari – Seema's village – was even closer, only nine kilometres from the epicentre, and was completely flattened, like many villages in Kutch. More than 70 per cent of buildings in Kutch were destroyed.

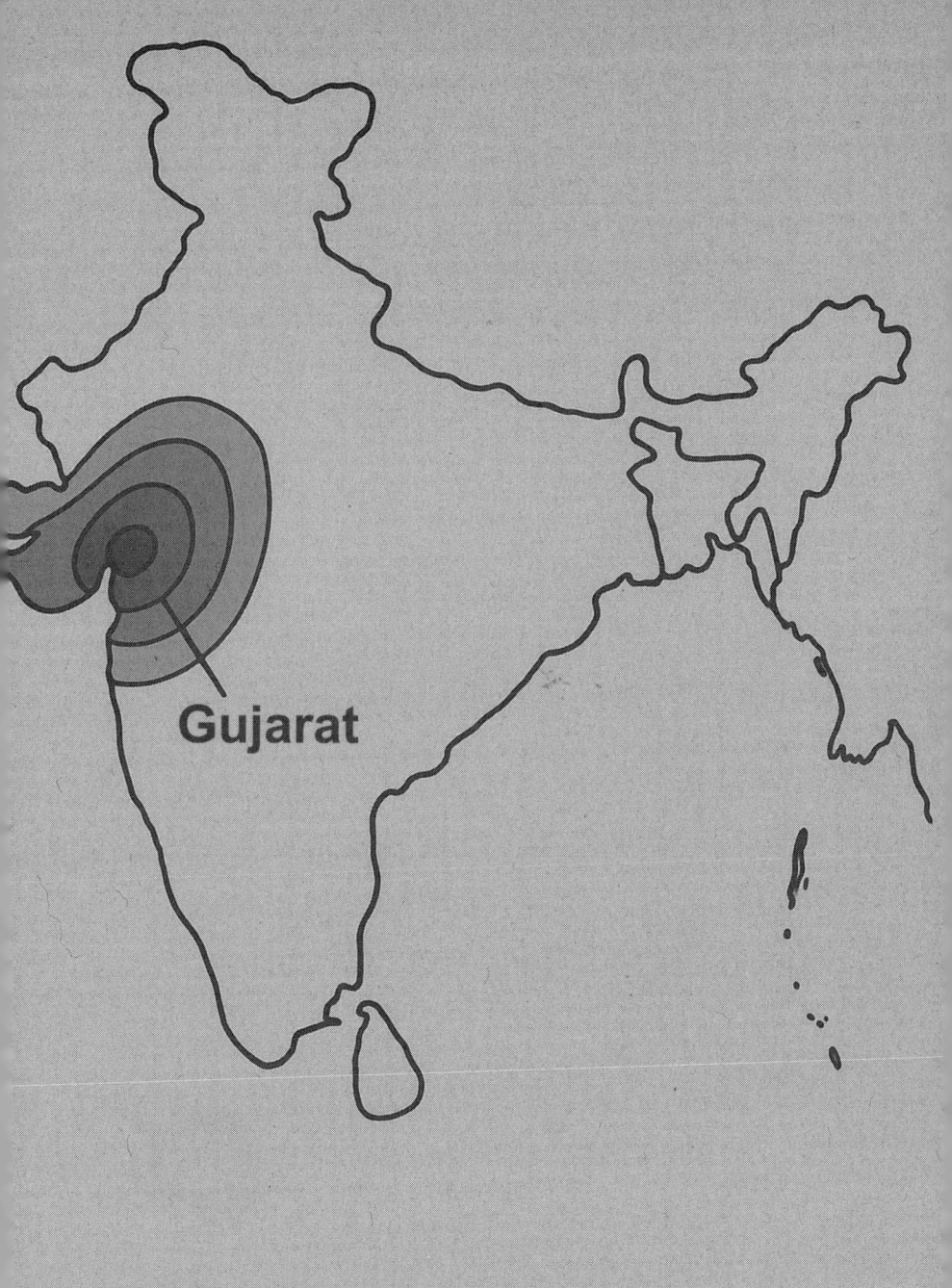

People in Gujarat already knew about disasters. Before 2001, they had had cyclones and two years of severe drought. Many who listened to Seema were survivors of one disaster or another. Some remembered the Anjar Earthquake of 1956, like Nana.

Seema also learned about social capital – a fancy term about the benefits of people trusting each other, working together and helping their neighbours. In Kutch, social capital was strong. It helped the area recover faster. Thousands of children were lost or got separated from their parents. Many were cared for by the community, NGOs, religious groups and kind people, not just by the government. In villages, neighbours often took in children, especially if no relatives could be found. That is what happened with Arjan.

When Seema spoke, the quietest moment always came when she described what she had done the second the ground had begun to roar: she and Padma had dived under the

bed – with water, food and a flashlight. People were amazed that a small girl did the right thing while everything fell down.

'How did you think of that?' they asked. 'Weren't you scared?'

Seema said, 'My Nana had told us to be prepared. So, I tried to be. And I prayed to Mother Durga to protect us.'

People nodded. 'She honours her grandfather,' some said. 'She honours the goddess,' others added.

Seema also explained how Nana had built their house: he had used strong mud blocks, strengthened the walls, chosen a good site and made a strong foundation. She spoke about how she had worked with the NGO to rebuild – and how they had even improved on Nana's methods.

The NGO worker was thrilled. Seema's talks reached more and more communities. Soon, she was known across NGOs as a strong voice for

bravery, helping people, villages and groups in Gujarat and beyond.

She spoke in classrooms, community centres, under banyan trees with elders and in fields with farmers. Months passed. She travelled across the state. She was 'the girl who survived' and also an expert on the Gujarat Earthquake and earthquake-safe building methods.

One day she noticed something: the nightmares were gone.

'Nani, why do you think that is?' Seema asked.

'I think the time for nightmares has passed, beti,' Nani said softly. 'Goddess Durga supports you and protects you now. She will not leave you, so nightmares cannot trouble you.'

Months became years. Seema kept studying – first in Chobari, then at the government high school in Bhuj – while still giving talks about being ready for disasters. She did very well in school: high marks, good debates, strong

presentations. She loved helping others and shared what she knew.

Her grades and her public speaking efforts caught the eye of universities and people in the state government. When it was time to choose a college, several schools invited her, including the famous Indian Institutes of Technology (IITs).

Seema wanted to stay in Gujarat near Nani, Padma and Arjan. But the newly established IIT Gandhinagar did not yet have civil engineering, which she wanted to study so she could design buildings that could withstand earthquakes, cyclones, floods, drought and heat. So, she made a tough choice to move away and went to Mumbai to study at IIT Bombay.

Today, Seema works for the Coalition for Disaster Resilient Infrastructure (CDRI) in New Delhi. It is an international group that helps make buildings and systems safer from climate change and natural disasters. And she kept her

promise to Padma – she took her to Delhi and showed her all the famous places.

Two sisters lived through the worst natural disaster in Gujarat's history – and one of India's worst. They survived because they were prepared and because their grandfather had built a strong house. They lost so much that day in January 2001, but they also gained a lot: a brother in Arjan, and a deep, steady strength inside.

They witnessed the 2001 Gujarat (Bhuj) Earthquake. And even now, when they see each other, they grin and call out:

'Be prepared!'

And they always are.

OTHER BOOKS IN THE SERIES

3 December 1984, Bhopal.

Vikram is sneaking back home after a night out with his friends when the sirens at the nearby gas factory start to wail. A strange, choking smell fills the air. Within minutes, the streets are a nightmare – people and animals lying on the ground, eyes red, mouths foaming. The stench of rotten cabbages hangs everywhere.

Terrified, Vikram wakes his little brother up. Together, they run into the dark night, trying to escape the invisible poison swirling through their city. But where can they go? And how far will they get before it's too late?

26 December 2004, Mahabalipuram.

Arun Soni and his family are enjoying a holiday by the sea. But the fun doesn't last long. The very next morning, Arun notices something strange – the ocean has pulled back, leaving the beach bare. Before anyone can understand what's happening, a roaring wall of water comes crashing in.

A giant tsunami slams into the shore, smashing their hotel and flooding their room. In an instant, Arun is swept out to sea, fighting against the monstrous waves. Alone, terrified and far from safety, can Arun find his way back to his family?